Sticky Summer Shorts

EXPLICIT GAY EROTICA

G.R. RICHARDS

Cover design © 2013 G.R. Richards
First Edition July 2013
ISBN-13: 978-1500554897
ISBN-10: 1500554898

Ebook version is available from Excessica Publishing

"A Scream in the Woods," "Brody and the Boy Bench," "Swimming in the Rain," "Daddy had a Boat," and "Click!" originally published by Constable and Robinson. "Poke on the Water" originally published by Torquere Press.

CONTENTS

DADDY HAD A BOAT

Normally, I wouldn't go for a silver daddy—but this guy was an easy exception. How could I say no? He had a boat!

Actually, he was pretty good-looking for a guy his age. You wouldn't have guessed he was in his fifties. Fifties! That meant, like, thirty years older than me. But, as I said, he was pretty fucking hot... and he had a boat.

Money's a turn-on, and anyone who says different is a big fat liar. Money's all about possibilities—food and booze and trips. And a boat, in my silver daddy's case.

We met when I took this short-term gig at the Outdoor Living trade show. My job was to wear a wetsuit and encourage people to sit on this new model of jet ski. I was Eye Candy Dude, working alongside Eye Candy Chick. She flirted with the straight guys, I flirted with the gay ones. Sex sells.

Come to think of it, Candy Chick was the one who turned me on to Louie. I remember saying, "No way that guy's gay. You take him."

And she was like, "Trust me—he hasn't looked at my tits once. He's all yours."

So, even though Louie didn't get my gaydar up, I trusted my co-conspirator's instinct. At first, he seemed like he was trying to brush me off. He didn't take a flyer and he didn't want to sit on the jet ski... but he didn't walk away, either. Something had piqued his interest, and it wasn't the product.

One thing led to another, and he ended up inviting me to his Harbourfront condo. A few of my friends lived in condos, but they were nothing special. Louie's place? Hey, "special" didn't even begin to describe it. Pure luxury. The best of everything. Enough room for a baby grand, and a view to die for—even at night.

Not just that, but as he plied me with drinks he happened to mention that he was "mostly retired" and only came into town once in a while. His "humble abode" in the city sat disused for weeks on end. He sighed like a total drama queen and said, "It's a shame I don't have a houseboy to take care of the place while I'm at the lake."

I'm no dummy. I jumped right on that, assuring him, "I can water the plants and keep the fridge stocked. Anything you need."

"Anything?" he asked, setting his wine glass down on the piano.

I was straining to see out the window when he approached me from behind. His image in the darkened glass seemed wolfish. Predatory. He looked like an entirely different person. I watched him in the window, a black mirror against the darkened harbour view. He took off his glasses, absently setting them on a built-in bookcase.

It was kind of a Clark Kent moment. Suddenly he was Superman. I mean, the guy was *hot*. His silver hair was like a white flame burning just for me. When he came a little closer I could feel his body heat blazing through my clothes. I'd changed out of my wetsuit, but I had a feeling my jeans and button-down top would be strewn across the Brazilian hardwood before long.

"You like what you see?" Louie asked.

That was a lame-ass come-on line, but his money spoke louder than words. I nodded without turning away from the window.

Pressing his front against my back, he asked, "Would you like another drink, Alexander?"

My throat was dry as sand, but I managed to squeak out, "No thanks."

He took my glass and set it on the bookcase. I couldn't think what to say, so I didn't say anything. I just watched his direct movements. He was so suave the heat of his breath brought my cock surging to life. Even reflected in the window, I could see fire in his eyes. He knew how much he turned me on. My dick pummelled the inside my jeans, begging for escape, and that man knew just what to do.

Louie kissed my neck sharply as he unbuttoned my top. His goatee stabbed my throat when he bit, but I loved it. There was something sophisticated yet unabashedly masculine about his meticulous beard. When he brushed it up and down my neck, I just wanted to throw him against the floor-to-ceiling window and launch my tongue down his throat.

But I didn't.

Men like Louie exercise control over guys like me, and I was totally willing to hand my power over to him.

I waited for Louie to turn me around. He kissed me sharply, crushing his mouth to mine, drawing the breath from my lungs. I had no choice but to breathe with him, rely on his every inhale and exhale to sustain me. Every burst of oxygen got my heart pumping more blood to my already massive erection. I wondered what he wanted to do with me. Should I wait? Should I ask?

Louie drew away, leaving me stumbling and dizzy. He picked up his wine glass and sat on the piano bench, then said, "Strip for me."

"Strip?" I asked. My ears were ringing as I struggled to breathe on my own. I felt weirdly confused, even though his request wasn't unusual.

"Strip *for me*," he clarified. There was a difference. A guy like Louie could own anything and anyone. He could own me, if I let him.

There'd been music piping through the stereo the whole time, but I didn't really notice until that moment. Dirty jazz. Perfect.

"This feels kind of weird," I said. Yeah, I knew

how to play this game. I wasn't stupid. "Would you believe I've never stripped for anyone?"

"Not for a second," he said, raising a stern eyebrow. His gaze was so piercing I could have pissed my pants. Then he let out a hearty laugh, and sweet relief flooded my veins. I'd only just met this guy. He could be a total nut job, for all I knew.

But he was undeniably wealthy, so what choice did I have? I put on a show. Shrugging my shirt off my shoulders, I let it tumble to the floor.

"Very nice," Louie said. A vicious grin spread across his lips. "Delicious abs."

The compliment struck me to the core, but all I could muster was a flimsy, "Thanks."

I unbuckled my belt slowly, swaying to the music. Louie hissed as he watched. He didn't take his eyes off my hips. They swung like a pendulum, side to side, and when he was good and hypnotized I slid my belt from its loops in one flagrant display. It became my whip and I cracked it across the room just to make that sound: *whhh-chkh, whhh-chkh*.

"Impressive," he said. His voice was deeper now, more of a growl. "Will I be so impressed when you take off those trousers? That *is* the question."

I chuckled, trying to stay coy, but once I'd taken it all off I started feeling cocky. I danced around the room for my silver daddy, watching his eyes bug out. That's right. I had a dick to die for.

Now I was hard and ready, and just waiting for Louie to tell me what to do.

He surprised me by sitting on the leather couch all the way across the room. When he told me to stand in front of the window, I felt a little weird about it. All the lights were on. Never know who might catch a glimpse of my naked body. But I couldn't say no. The lust in my new silver daddy's eyes spurred me on.

I stood in front of the great window and pressed my back against the glass, writhing to the dirty jazz. It felt good knowing someone out there might see my ass pressed against the window as I danced. I felt like such a fucking slut that I started touching myself all over, running my hands up and down my chest, avoiding my aching cock even though I wanted to touch it most of all. I knew how to build suspense.

And it worked. From the other side of the room, Louie shouted, "Stroke your fucking cock, twink!"

Finally I had permission! I wrapped my fist around my throbbing shaft, feeling the vein at its base pulsing against my palm. Tightening my grip, I stroked my dick nice and slow, just for daddy Louie.

I could tell how much he love watching me, because he sneered and snapped, "Spit on your dick."

So I did. I opened my hand and lowered my head and released a clear stream of hot saliva. Louie told me to rub it into my cockhead, so I did, tracing my thumb around my red-hot tip as he watched.

I sort of wondered why he hadn't come over, why he was so far away, why he wasn't fucking my ass or anything. His mouth around my cock? Wow, that would be something. But the more I stroked myself off, the more I knew he wasn't coming over.

Daddy liked to watch.

So I throttled my dick just for him. I pressed my shoulder blades against the window and hoped it wouldn't break with my weight. My cock begged me to take it over the edge, and I told Louie, "I need to come."

He said no. No, I couldn't, not here. I had to wait.

Wait for what?

Oh God, my dick was aching so bad it actually hurt. My cockhead wasn't even red anymore, it was purple now, and it needed to explode. I wanted to come all over the bookshelf, or fill my wine glass with jizz. It was sitting right there! I could just grab it and stroke off real hard and fill that gaping goblet with hot cream.

Louie finally got up from the couch. For a second I thought he'd make my dreams come true and wrap his mouth around my dick. Nope. He stood a good five feet away, still fully dressed, and told me to turn around.

I swallowed hard as I faced the dark window. There was my reflection, there was his behind me. His eyes burned dark as the devil. Why wouldn't he let me come? I'd done everything he wanted. And I was ready. God, was I ready!

It felt like a million years had gone by when he finally said, "Ejaculate! Come all over my window."

He didn't have to ask twice. I fucked my hand until I burst, spraying thick ropes of cum down the glass. I'd barely finished spilling my jizz when my silver daddy told me to get on my knees. Just as well, because my legs felt too wobbly to stand.

Once I was on my knees, Louie's hand found its way to the back of my head and he forced my face close to the glass. My heart raged, and if I hadn't just come I'm sure I would have been hard again.

"Clean it up," he instructed, and I got on it quick. Nothing worse than cold cream. I licked the glass, swallowing mouthfuls of my own hot cum. It tasted faintly of Windex and I could only hope that stuff wasn't too toxic.

When I'd licked up every last trace, I bowed my head and waited. Louie hadn't gotten off. What did he have planned for me?

But my silver daddy took a step back and sat on the piano bench. He asked me to turn and face him. I knelt before him and looked up at the splendor of his richness. There was nothing sexier than a guy with money. Nothing.

Louie asked if I'd like to take care of his condo while he was away, and I jumped off the ground, wrapping my arms around him. I would have done anything, and I told him so, but he didn't ask for more. I thought that was a little weird, but everyone gets off on something different and if Louie liked to watch, who was I to criticize?

I don't know why he trusted me so fast. He didn't ask for references or anything, just gave me a set of keys and told me what to do clean and water and stock the fridge with.

At first, I was really well-behaved. I didn't want to lose this gig. Louie's condo was amazing, and such a great retreat from my ratty apartment and all my asshole roommates. I started sleeping in silver daddy's bed, even though he'd told me not too. The mattress was like a cloud, so comfortable. I slept like a baby there.

And then it was my friend Julia's twenty-first birthday and I wanted to do something special because she was so awesome when my parents kicked me out. Louie said no parties and no friends, but seriously? It's not like we were going to trash the place.

Okay, well the party got way bigger than I could handle, and soon my cheap-ass beer wasn't good enough and everybody was raiding Louie's liquor cabinet. When I told them to leave the stuff alone, they kept saying, "Don't worry, daddy won't mind." I'd never heard the word "daddy" so many times in my life, and they said it like an insult.

The very next morning, when I was hung over and

left alone to clean up the mess, Louie's driver knocked at the door. He had a note for me. I was to get in the car and he'd drive me to the lake. He could obviously see over my shoulder, see how my friends had obliterated the condo, but he made no reaction. What could I do? I got in the limo and cracked a hair-of-the-dog Heineken.

I wasn't too worried. Louie probably had a craving to see me jerk off. He really liked to watch.

Turned out I had no idea how much he liked to watch. The guy had surveillance cameras set up all over the condo. He'd been watching me the whole time. He'd seen Julia's party. He'd seen everything.

Louie told me all this when I got to the lake. The driver walked me around to the back of the huge lake house, where Louie's boat was docked. At first Louie was totally casual, like nothing was going on. He acted all happy to see me and everything. He said we were going for a little ride.

When we were out on the water and the lake house was just a spot on the horizon, that's when he confessed he'd been watching me for weeks.

How could I respond? It was his condo. I'd broken the rules. I just apologized over and over, hoping he'd keep me on as houseboy or whatever the hell I was.

"Daddy's very upset with you," he said, and at first that confused me because he'd never referred to himself that way before. It must have been because all my stupid friends were calling him that.

Anyway, I just went with it. I could play any game.

I said, "I'm sorry, Daddy. I was bad. How do you want to punish me?"

He took his glasses off and squinted against the sun. Then he pointed to the front of the boat, whatever that's called, and said, "Get naked and get out there."

What? I was all for exhibitionism, but stand naked at the front of a moving boat? Anyone might see me! That is, if I didn't fall off and drown first. The things we do for men with money! Louie slowed the boat down while I stripped, and his wolfish grin egged me on. I was hard already. Maybe I was more of an exhibitionist than I wanted to believe.

I said a little prayer as Louie helped me over the windshield type thing in front of the wheel. Even his goddamn boat had leather seats! The craft was still moving when I walked out onto the fibreglass front. It was white, but it still burned my feet. I screeched in pain, trying not to jump because I was sure I'd put both feet through the boat.

It wasn't smooth sailing. It wasn't steady. The craft kept rocking as it carved a path through the calm lake. Thank God I was a master of subway surfing, or I'd never have managed to stay upright. All the same, I was convinced I was going to die.

Louie shouted at me to turn around and I called back, "Yes Daddy," but it took me the better part of five minutes to actually do it. I was still hard, half with arousal and half with fear, when he told me to get on my knees. That was a relief, though it wasn't easy. Nothing is easy when you're scared shitless and rocking the boat.

When I finally managed to get down on my knees, Louie told me to fuck my hand. I guess I shouldn't have been surprised, but I was. All I wanted to do was put both hands down and get some sense of relief...but I guess release would have to do.

Staring at my reflection in Louie's sunglasses, I grabbed my dick. The sun was hot against my skin and I suddenly got really afraid of burning my special area. That's why I wrapped both hands around my fat cock and stroked it within the hot suction of my fingers. Fuck, that felt amazing.

Louie sped up and I planted my knees against the boat. My heart raced and my erection pulsed in my hands. I couldn't tell if I was too scared to come, or if it would happen right away. I'd never been on a boat before.

As we picked up speed, cool droplets of water misted my back. The lake was after me. It pummelled my naked ass like rain, and considering how hot the day was, it actually felt good. I worked my dick harder. Both hands pumping. Fuck, it felt incredible. I watched Louie's mouth as I jerked off. His sneer made me want to jizz all over his face. I kept picturing thick ropes of cum dripping from his dark glasses onto his lips.

"Come for Daddy!" he shouted. It was hard to hear over the hum of the engine and the searing spray of water, but I did as I was told. Coming for Louie was easy.

I sprayed my jizz across the front of the boat, and it disappeared, white on white. Once it had left my body it was gone. Thank God Louie didn't want me to lick it up, because I'd never have found it. Still, the idea of licking my hot jizz from the searing boat made my dick twinge just a little bit.

Louie slowed the boat down and cut the engine. The quiet on the lake was almost scary, and when he asked me if I could swim I was sure that was the end of me. Then he peeled off his polo shirt and khaki shorts and he jumped in the water wearing nothing but a speedo. I joined him and the lake was cold enough to rouse me from my orgasmic stupor.

Suddenly I felt more alive than ever. I thought about jerking off totally naked on the front of a moving boat, and my spent cock wanted to get hard again.

Daddy Louie splashed me. I laughed and splashed him back. He asked if I'd learned my lesson and I said no, probably not. He just laughed, and I knew we understood each other.

"You're young," he said. "You're bound to do stupid things."

I said, "You can punish me any way you want, any time you want."

And he sure took me up on that offer.

A SCREAM IN THE WOODS

Primal Therapy was big in the 70's. Kids today have probably never heard of this hippie stuff, but John Lennon really popularized it back in the day. The thinking was that we all had childhood trauma we needed to let out before we could grow into sane and stable human beings.

For some reason, my wife decided this therapy was something I could use. I told her I wasn't traumatized, but she said I could be so "difficult" at times... whatever that means. She said a friend from work had sent her husband off on this scream retreat in the woods. It was all men there. They camped under the stars and caught their own food, cooked on open flames. A lot of chest-beating and letting loose, my wife told me. "And more." I didn't fully comprehend the weight of those two little words until I was out in the forest with a group of guys.

They were amiable enough. I figured the group would be full of neurotic nerds, but they were mostly guys like me. Our wives had probably all conspired to get us out of the house for the weekend. One guy joked that they were at home in a naked writhing mass, enjoying a lesbian sex party.

My cock pulsed in my pants when I pictured my wife with her face between a smooth set of thighs. I'd be mad as hell if she fucked another man, but it wouldn't bother me in the least if she wanted a taste of pussy. Especially if she let me watch.

While we built lean-tos out of fallen branches and fresh fern, I told the other guys what I was thinking. Hey, this was a therapy weekend after all. They all agreed that they'd gladly share their wives with willing women.

Maury, the leader of the group, asked about the flip-side: would our wives be upset if we sucked cock or fucked another man's ass? The question turned me numb. I had trouble even processing it.

All the guys started saying, "What? I would never do that! I'm no queer." I guess I joined in. I said that stuff too, even though... well, I wasn't as sure as they seemed to be.

Maury insisted it was a hypothetical question: what would our wives think? Would they be upset if we queered out on them? Would they think it was hot? Would they want to watch, or take a "boys will be boys" attitude and just ignore it?

That actually got us talking more in-depth, speculating on what our wives imagined we were like on the inside. Sometimes Josie acted like I had no feelings just because I didn't share every emotion with her or cry during corny movies. She probably thought sex was the only thing that was ever on my mind.

All the guys seemed to agree with that. Some said sex *was* the most important thing in the world, and they wished their wives would let loose a bit more. Two of the guys said they'd lost interest in sex completely. They just couldn't be bothered anymore. Others confessed to paying prostitutes for the pleasure—and not just female prostitutes.

The group went quiet, then, until one of the sexless guys asked what it was like. The guy who answered was big and burly like a football star. He said you could be rough with other men. It wasn't about love or romance or anything like that. Pure physical lust—pure satisfaction. When he took another man's ass, he was in complete control. He could go crazy, no holding back. He'd arch the guy over or bend him against a tree, take hold of his hips, and just fuck the life out of him. That was manly sex.

After that, we went hunting. Not with guns, though. Maury told us to run around the forest like animals. We should howl, we should stalk our prey, and anything we could catch with our bare hands or decommission with a big stick or a rock, we could eat. If we caught nothing, we'd eat nothing.

Some of the guys went out in a pack, but I was a lone wolf. I chased hares through the forest like an idiot. It felt good to run and dive at my prey. It felt good to howl as a warning and then scream in frustration. I'd never realized how much pent-up frustration I had until I started letting it out.

By the time I got back to camp, all the other guys were busy prepping their meat for stew. Maury had brought some carrots, potatoes and onions to throw in, and dinner was prepared in a big metal pot over the fire. Thank god they shared with me, because I was starving.

After dinner, we sat around the fire in a stupor, staring into the flames. I got nervous because I was sure Maury was going to start the "therapy" then. Everything we'd done so far had been really neat, and I didn't want to ruin it with guys crying about how their mothers never loved them enough.

Luckily, that's not what happened. Maury turned his face to the moon and howled. So did I. We all did. It felt amazing, like singing in a choir. A chorus of men. We howled and screamed and barked so much I got light-headed. I felt mesmerized and impressionable, like my body and mind were different entities.

Something happened, then. I still can't say how it started. All I know is that Trevor stood up first—that's the guy who'd talked about paying guys to fuck. He tore out of his jeans and plaid shirt, standing naked so the fire painted his flesh orange. Like Tarzan, he beat his chest and roared. It was scary and exciting and it made my dick hard as wood.

Trevor was a big guy in every sense. His shoulders were huge and so were his arms. His stomach was jagged with muscles. He looked like some kind of bodybuilder. And then there was his dick. It hung between his slightly parted thighs like a thick sausage in a butcher shop window.

Even though I'd just eaten dinner, my mouth watered for meat. But Trevor had his eyes on another prize: Arthur, the lankiest of those few men who'd lost all interest in sex.

To be honest, I can't remember if words were spoken. It all happened in a haze. Arthur stripped bare. He was a skinny-ass guy with a moustache—we all had moustaches in those days—but the orange glaze painted across his skin by the flames made him look a lot less pasty than he otherwise would.

His dick wasn't hard. Arthur fell to his knees, facing away from me, but I couldn't help straining to stare at the thing hanging between his legs, set on a cushion of hairy balls. I wondered if the guy would get off. I wondered if he'd be turned on by another man.

Trevor ran his hand through Arthur's white-guy 'fro, latching onto waves of auburn hair. The guy's head snapped back a touch and I wondered if it hurt. Arthur didn't seem to mind. Everyone was watching and he didn't say a word.

That huge sausage between Trevor's thighs perked up. He grabbed it by the root, whacking its mushroom tip against Arthur's lips. I strained and bent to get a good look as the big guy slid his ferocious dick into the little guy's mouth.

Arthur choked on it. He gagged as Trevor buried that meaty monster at the back of his throat. Still, he didn't fight. He was naked, but he didn't struggle or try to get away, or say no—not that he could have gotten much sound out with a big dick ramming his gullet.

I don't think I blinked the whole time this was happening. Everybody seemed mesmerized by the unexpected sex show. It was so brutal, so raw, and yet Arthur was a willing victim. Even his dick started reacting while Trevor pounded his throat. It got huge, got hard, and it stood up naked, pointing up at the man with the big guns.

When I felt a hand on my shoulder, I just about jumped out of my jeans. I was so caught up in Trevor and Arthur that I'd lost track of the world.

The hand belonged to Maury, our group leader. It wasn't just sitting there doing nothing. No, he was rubbing my shoulder, warming my tight muscles even through the thickness of my lumberjack shirt. The night had gotten cool when the sun went down. Now, with the fire roaring and Arthur going down on Trevor, a strange heat rose through my thighs. My balls felt tight. My dick strained against the fly of my tough blue jeans.

Then Maury asked me something that made me cringe: "How does that make you feel?"

Ugh! What a *therapist* question.

I shrugged hard, trying to brush his hand off my shoulder. I said, "I don't know. Good, I guess."

His hand moved off my shoulder, which in a way was a relief, but in another way made me regret being harsh with him. I started unbuttoning my plaid shirt without really noticing. I assured myself I was just doing it because I was hot. Nothing about wanting to get naked, wanting to fuck another man, or suck someone off. I was just overheated from sitting so close to the fire.

I looked around. My heart just about stopped when realized all the guys in the group had paired up. This wasn't in the brochure!

As much as I wanted to be shocked and appalled, I was in such a dreamy state that all I felt was aroused. My dick thudded against my fly so hard that, when Maury wrapped his arms around my waist and undid my pants, I almost thought my erection had done it.

Maury found my cock effortlessly, pulling it out and stroking my thick shaft. I was perched on a log, and I could tell he was kneeling on the ground behind it, but I didn't turn around. It would be better if things just happened without me noticing too much. Then it would all be like a dream, like I didn't intend it, and then it wouldn't be cheating. I loved my wife. I wouldn't do anything to hurt her.

When Maury stood up, I took over rubbing my cock. I couldn't stop. It felt too good. He stepped over the log and unbuckled his belt, unzipped his fly. His cock shot out of there like a cannon all ready to blow. His lanky body blocked my view of the fire, but I could still see Trevor fucking Arthur's throat out of the corner of my eye. The sight made my cock throb against my palm.

Maury's naked cock pulsed right in front of my face. I didn't know what to do. I wanted to wrap my lips around that veiny monster and suck until he came, but something held me back.

"Do it," he said. "It's okay."

When I looked into his eyes, I realized my wife had planned all this. It wasn't therapy, but something even more primal: men fucking men. Men sucking men. I'd been sent to the woods to get off with other guys, and the idea that my wife was at home imagining all this turned me on so hard I almost jizzed on my fingers.

Diving at Maury's dick, I swallowed him whole, choking when his cockhead met the back of my throat.

He kept encouraging me, saying it was okay. I backed off for a moment and gazed around the fire pit. The guys in the group had taken up all different positions. Some were sitting, others hunched over with their faces buried in another man's crotch. Some stood like Maury, others kneeled like Arthur. One guy was laid out along a log like a virgin sacrifice. Two half-naked men growled and fought over his erection, taking it in turns, deep-throating until they gagged.

I looked up at the group leader. His genuine expression warmed me. He obviously wanted to help men become fulfilled and happy. In that sense, he reminded me of my wife—that same deep caring, but in a vastly different body. For a second, I pictured what my beautiful bride would look like if she had a cock like Maury's. I imagined her naked, with those sweet, pendulous breasts supported by a nice satin bra. I imagined kissing a path down the curve of her belly and finding this hefty slab of man meat. A big cock right there at the apex of her thighs.

Leaning forward, I took Maury's pulsing tip between my lips. It was hotter than hell, but soft as silk sheets. I played with his cockhead, making a tight O with my lips and teasing that ridge where tip met shaft. He ran his hand through my hair and moaned softly. I guess he liked it.

Maury could obviously tell how jealous I felt that he was getting all the pleasure. He forced me down on the log until I was lying like that other guy. He shoved his dick in my mouth, but not too hard. When I had him between my lips, I sucked to keep him in place. It was like tasting the scent of my own dick.

Bending us into a sixty-nine position, Maury sucked my dick into his mouth. The leader worked me and I worked him. Just mouths, no hands. Every time I started choking, he eased up, and I appreciated that. He sucked me hard, then soft, alternating the sensations, kissing my balls, biting my shaft. I couldn't manage any of that stuff. I had a hard enough time concentrating on his fierce erection as it pounded my throat.

When I came, I didn't see it coming. I'd filled his mouth with jizz before I even felt that familiar tightening in my balls. I guess my eruption turned Maury on, because he came moments later.

I gagged on his cum. There was so much of it, and it tasted so weird—sweet and tangy and rancid all at once—that my throat expelled it. I spat cream all over his dick and my face. It was everywhere.

As I looked around the dwindling fire, there were a few guys still going, but most were done and covered in cum. Trevor sat on a log with his naked legs wide open and Arthur sitting between them. Both guys were staring into the fire with silly, happy grins plastered across their faces. The scene was priceless.

Maury sat beside me, but he didn't say anything. I was glad about that. I thought about my wife, about how much I loved her, and how truly and deeply touched I was that she'd set this up. I had no idea how badly I needed a weekend of man-on-man sucking and fucking.

Wives are always right.

CLICK!

Barry waited where the guy said he'd be: the field northeast of the cloverleaf at Dixon Road and the 401. Strange place for a photo shoot, with all those cars driving up the onramp and the overhead noise from the nearby airport.

Judging from the online ad, this was bound to be a strange session. Not that he had any other photo shoots to compare this one to. That was another strange thing—what kind of photographer hired a model who blatantly confessed he had no experience whatsoever?

The kind of photographer, it turned out, who needed his models to work pro bono.

Oh well. Barry'd been working out all summer, and he could finally look in the mirror and feel pleased with the man looking back at him.

The photographer's name was Paul. Barry didn't want to forget, so he'd written it on a blank piece of paper, which turned out to have his phone bill on the other side. He'd have to remind himself to pay that–it was already past due. It's not that Barry didn't have the money, just that he'd never been good with the details. That's why he'd written Paul's name down. Details.

"Hey!"

Barry turned to see a kid jogging toward him in black jeans, a black fitted T, and lightweight purple and blue checked scarf. He looked like a perfect anomaly in the waist-high grasses, which had gone to seed and looked like a field of wheat. Maybe that's why the kid had chosen this location. Barry could play the farm hand in the field.

Glancing down at the name he'd scrawled on paper, Barry asked, "Paul?"

"Yeah," the kid said. "You're Barry?"

Paul shook Barry's hand before tossing a black backpack to the ground. What had he gotten himself into this time?

"Are you just coming from school?" Barry asked. As soon as the words left his mouth, he realized it was August and there was no school.

"Yeah right," Paul said. "Don't I wish!"

The longer Barry looked at Paul, the older he appeared. Maybe it was just his lanky body and the awkward way he moved that made him appear young. His skin was pale and his cheeks somewhat sallow, but his dark, messy hair compensated by giving him the look of an artist.

"How long have you been taking pictures?" Barry asked, just to make conversation.

Paul blinked. Twice. "Uh..."

"Oh..."

"Okay, so, here's the thing..." Paul began by taking a Sliver Elf Digital from the back pocket of his skinny jeans.

"That's your camera?" Barry laughed. He didn't mean to come off like such a jackass, but any photographer worth his salt should have a better camera than that. Damn, his niece had an Elf Digital, and she was seven!

Scratching his head, Paul looked at Barry. "Okay, so, I'm trying to get into art school, right? But I didn't know you had to do all this stuff..."

"Then you *are* a student?" Barry felt misled. He thought this would be something serious, or at least a good way to spend a hot Sunday afternoon.

Paul started to answer, but a plane flew by overhead. They were too close to the airport to talk over its roar. When it had cast its dark shadow across them and moved on, Paul said, "I *was* a student. I figured I'd make my parents proud and become the great gay mathematician. But then I got to university and..." Scrunching his pale nose, he said, "It was hard!"

"Okay..." Barry offered a shrug he hoped would convey: *Relevance?*

"Well, I failed. It was like math at university was different from math in high school. So I figured screw math, I'll go to art college. But do you know all the bullshit they put you through just to apply? You have to write essays and put together a portfolio and..." He trailed off, looking around the overpass. Holding his camera up, he said, "I was thinking fashion photography, or, like...nudes...?"

The inflection in Paul's voice went up in time with Barry's cock. That word, *nudes*, answered the question he hadn't wanted to ask. Ever since he saw Paul's request for a model online, he'd hoped...well, he didn't want to jinx it. Maybe Paul didn't mean what Barry thought he meant.

"I can get naked," Barry said. Then he looked around, too. "Oh...the cars...do you think...?"

"How would they know?" Paul asked. "I mean, they're off in the distance, they're not looking this way, and, anyway, this grass comes right up to your..."

"Yeah..."

They both looked around. Barry took a moment to second-guess himself before tearing out a piece of long grass and sticking it in his mouth like a farm boy.

"I can't pay you," Paul said.

Barry nodded. "I know. But, hey, you're applying for art college, right? I always wanted to go, so I'm happy to help." He started unbuttoning his shirt, and then wondered if he should wait for instructions. "Did you wanna tell me what to do?"

"Oh, yeah, I guess I should." Paul laughed. He sounded nervous, poor kid. "Yeah, take off your shirt and turn around. I want to get some shots of your back."

As per instruction, Barry turned away and stripped off his shirt. This was the first time he could remember taking off his clothes in public and being happy another man's eyes were on him. For a good long time, he wouldn't even like to take his top off at the beach. He'd always felt chunky. That's why he bought work-out equipment instead of joining a gym. The thought of all those attractive young guys seeing his blubbery body destroyed his last vestiges of self-assurance.

But now things were different. He'd worked tirelessly at improving his body. Now, even with his back to Paul, Barry knew the young guy was smiling. He could feel that grin burning into his skin, hotter than the August sun. When he didn't hear a click, he turned and asked, "What do you want me to do with my hands?"

Paul looked him straight in the eye, and blinked. Twice. It was beyond obvious the guy'd been staring at his ass. Barry tried not to smile too widely as Paul shook his head. "Huh? What did you say?"

A plane flew overhead, so Barry waited a moment

before asking, "Where should I put my arms? Do you want me to pose, or should I just do what comes naturally?"

He could feel Paul's stare drizzling like hot caramel down his strong shoulders.

"Can you make your hands into fists?" Paul asked. "Set them on your hips, then look up to the sky, like Superman."

Barry chuckled at the image of himself as Superman, but he posed while Paul click-click-clicked behind him. On a whim, he raised his fists to the sky like a first place runner who'd just crossed the finish line.

Paul cried, "Good! Good! Go with it."

The sun beat down on his chest, and Barry felt proud as hell. He wanted his abs commemorated in their current state, before his body went to pot again. Every sinew and bulge must be recorded for posterity. He turned around and watched as Paul lowered the camera and stared. "Wow. I sure am glad you answered my ad."

With a rush of pride, Barry kicked off his jeans. "Me too."

Paul clicked a few shots, and then lowered his camera again. He looked like he was about to say something, but he didn't. And then a transport truck zoomed by and it was nearly as loud as the planes.

"Want another pose?" Barry asked. He wasn't sure how to stand anymore.

The photographer's chest rose to heaven and fell to hell. "Could you touch yourself? Through your underwear, I mean. Grip it with your fist and be like, *yeah, that's my cock.* Want a piece of me?" Then Paul quickly added, "Only if you want to. It's okay if you don't."

"Oh, I want to," Barry chuckled. And suddenly he knew just what to do. As Paul snapped picture after picture, Barry looked to the sky. Grabbing his package, he gave it a healthy squeeze. "Is this good?"

"Oh my god, it's great!" Paul cried. "Fuck, you look fantastic!"

"Yeah?" Barry asked, tracing his palm down his chest. "What if I do this?"

He watched Paul's jaw drop as he snuck his hand beneath his shorts. The thought of grabbing himself in front of Paul—and in front of the camera—aroused him more than anything in recent memory. Firsts were always like that, and this was a first in so many ways: he'd never been photographed nude before, and he'd never gotten naked in public.

"Take your shorts off," Paul said, "but slowly. Build anticipation."

Barry's erection had grown so big he could barely conceal it in his jockeys. His tip wanted to pop out from under the waistband every time he pulled down on the elastic. All the same, he turned and pulled his shorts down, showing Paul some ass before bringing them back up. Overtop of his black underwear, he cupped his package with both hands and let the muscles in his arms surge for the camera.

"Oh, yeah," Paul said, like he couldn't believe this was really happening. "Take 'em off. Just take 'em off. Give me some cock."

Without hesitation, Barry pushed his shorts down to his ankles and kicked them into his pile of clothes. He felt almost criminal, standing naked in the overgrown grass beside the highway. That feeling of wrongdoing only made his erection harder. He held it steady for the camera. "Are you getting good shots of this bad boy?"

Paul chuckled. "Oh yeah, baby. Nothing but."

"You want me to stroke it for the camera?"

Taking picture after picture, Paul said, "Stroke it for *me*."

Barry extended one hand toward the camera, as if to say, "Get over here and suck this monster!" He stroked his shaft from base to tip, going slow, making the same gesture again and again. Finally, he wrapped his thumb and four fingers firmly around the ridge of his cockhead.

"Are you getting this?" he asked Paul.

"All that precum you're pumping out? Yeah, the camera loves it." He chuckled. "So do I."

"You want a taste?" Barry asked.

He asked because he knew the answer, and without hesitation, Paul fell to his knees in the tall grass. Snapping photos of himself from every angle, he wrapped his pink lips around Barry's cock.

Barry tossed his head back as his balls quaked. A stranger was sucking his cock, and taking pictures of the whole thing. It seemed so unwise. They could end up anywhere. But Barry didn't give a fuck. Hell, he *hoped* those pics would end up online or in magazines. He hoped millions of guys would jerk off gazing at that shot of him clutching his balls, or this one of Paul devouring his dick.

Running a hand through Paul's dark hair, Barry held him in place. Paul took pictures from below while Barry fucked his face. The kid wasn't even sucking anymore, just taking Barry's thrusts like a warm receptacle. Paul squealed and whinnied, but Barry didn't slow his pace. He held Paul's face between his hands and plunged his prick inside that pretty little mouth. When his thighs began to shake, Paul pulled away.

Barry stared down at him from above while a plane flew by overhead. When its thundering roar had passed, he said, "I'm sorry. Was that too much?"

Paul's eyes darkened as he rose to his feet. "Get on the ground. Get on your knees and lean back on one elbow. Stick your chest up to the sky while you jack it, and when you come, come hard. I want a quality money shot."

The conniving smirk on Paul's face made Barry eager to please. He hoped he would come like a fountain, six feet in the air. Following Paul's instruction, he got on the ground. Grass sprang up like tiny prison bars all around him.

Paul clicked repeatedly while Barry fucked his hand. In Paul's smile, he could see how hot he looked. He could see the August sweat dripping down his chest, and his tan muscles gleaming as he tugged hard on his meat. He worked it fast, until his muscles began to twitch and his balls began to twinge. Then he worked it even faster, until finally the wave consumed him.

When he raised his hips to the sky, cum shot through the air in an ageless stream of white. Paul clicked like crazy as Barry's body convulsed, sending up torrents of cream until he was utterly exhausted.

Paul didn't stop taking pictures when Barry lay back in the sun. "This is the most elusive sensation there is," Paul said, clicking away. "This feeling of total relaxation. It's impossible to replicate, and pretty hard to capture, but the expression of bliss on your face says it all."

After a long while of lying underneath the airplanes and the August sun, Barry picked up his clothes and dressed. "So, good luck with your art school application and all that."

"Thanks," Paul chuckled. "But maybe I could skip

that step and go straight to shooting porn. What do you think?"

Barry reflected. "Good plan. And when you get there, give me a call. I've got a pretty good body, and anything's better than office work."

POKE ON THE WATER

The sky had been dark with rain all morning, and the sun was just now peeking out from behind the clouds. Even though it was past noon, it seemed early when Theo spotted Afi and Juan carrying the canoe down to the dock.

Theo slipped his flip flops onto his feet and ran from the cottage that he and seven friends had rented for the week. He didn't mean to let the screen door slam shut behind him, but he had to catch those guys before they set off on the water.

"Hey, hey, hey!" Theo cried from the hilly path to the dock. He was out of breath before he'd even reached the clearing. "Hey, guys. Going for a paddle? Can I come too?"

Yes, Theo realized how desperate he sounded, but at this point he didn't care. The whole reason he'd paid out his three hundred bucks to come on this trip was to spend a little time with Afi. He never imagined Juan would spend every moment of the retreat cock-blocking him. Afi and Juan had a crazy-bad breakup three years ago. Why the hell were they so chummy all of a sudden?

Afi and Juan stared blank-faced at Theo before tossing glances back and forth. "There are only the two seats," Juan finally said.

"That's fine by me." Theo didn't miss a beat. "I'll just ride on that wooden rung in the middle."

Afi kicked a leaf from the wet dock. It landed softly on the surface. The water was calm now. "Well, the thing is, we only have two paddles."

"Perfect!" Theo said. "Juan and I can paddle, and you can just relax. Or we could all take turns. Your call."

A smile broke across Juan's lips to complement the light bulb above his head. "Oh, we don't have a lifejacket for you! Too bad! Wouldn't want you to drown…"

Theo felt their resistance, but he wouldn't be beaten by it. "No worries. I worked as a lifeguard all through high school. If we flip, I'll manage."

Juan was obviously getting desperate. Theo could see it in his eyes. "But what if the canoe flips, hits you on the head, and knocks you unconscious? What then?"

This was getting ridiculous. With a shrug, Theo said, "Then I guess I'll die. Now come on, let's get this boat on the water while the sky is blue."

The guys seemed to be out of arguments, because they slunk to the ends of the canoe and slid it into the lake. A pool of minnows scattered in the clear brown water when the boat slipped in with barely a plunk. Theo stepped gingerly into the middle of the craft— okay, not the manliest way to get into a canoe, but he didn't want to flip the damn thing right off the bat.

Afi scratched the back of his bare leg with his big toe before slipping his foot back into his flip flop. Juan stood on the dock, legs spread, staring into the shallow water.

"Come on, guys," Theo called. "Pass me your paddles and get down here."

Tossing his knapsack and lifejacket into the boat, Juan set his paddle on the bottom of the canoe. He used it like a walking stick to step in. The craft sunk a bit on the back end and rocked side to side, but Theo held steady. Afi was looking at Juan when Theo extended a helping hand and guided him into the front.

"So, you're steering, Juan?" Theo and Afi took their seats.

"Am I?" Juan was a pampered big city boy. He obviously had no idea what he was doing in a canoe.

With Afi facing forward, Theo only got to stare at the back of his orange lifejacket, but that was better than letting him go off with Juan for yet another afternoon escapade. If they thought nobody noticed them always disappearing together, they were dead wrong. Theo noticed. "Sure you guys don't want me to paddle?" he asked.

Stupid question. "Hey, be my guest," Juan said, passing his paddle forward. "Steering sounds like more pressure than I can handle."

"Oh…" Theo really hadn't thought this offer through. Now they'd have to switch places, putting Juan closer to Afi. *Shit.* This vacation really wasn't working out the way he'd anticipated.

Rising to his feet with swaggering confidence, Theo set his paddle flat on the dock and clung to the wood as Juan came up behind him. Juan was even more unsteady on his feet than Theo. It gave Theo some satisfaction when Afi turned to watch his ex fumble and falter. He chuckled to himself until he felt the boat rock under his feet.

Juan hollered "Shit!" right before two strong arms wrapped themselves around Theo's middle. He could feel Juan's front pressed flush to his back, and Juan's face in the crook of his neck.

Never in his life had Theo felt so uncomfortable, irritated, and aroused all at the same time. And, judging by the stiffening bulge pressed into his ass crack and the hot, harsh breath on his cheek, Juan seemed to feel just the same way.

"I'm sorry," Juan said. "I almost fell."

"What are friends for?"

Of all the cottage renters, Juan seemed to like Theo the least. Maybe because he was so obviously interested in Afi. Juan always was the jealous type. That's why those two had broken up in the first place— Juan was too possessive and controlling. Theo would hate to see Afi go through that same shit all over again.

As he and Afi paddled across the wide open lake, Theo wondered if he might succeed in using the ex-couple's old issues to pry them apart. Only one way to find out, right?

Through the uncomfortable silence, he said, "So, Afi, remember when we went to that party for Glad Day and that guy from Kenya was, like, totally all over you? Didn't you go back to his place at the end of the night?"

"Yeah," Afi replied quickly.

Juan didn't seem too concerned, from what Theo could tell. Instead of provoking Juan's wrath, he'd only managed to embarrass Afi. Theo's stomach dropped into his flip flops. This vacation was not going well. Not just that, but Afi was barely dipping his paddles into the water. Theo was doing all the work and his muscles were killing him already.

They'd just reached the middle of the lake when Theo pulled his paddle from the shimmering water. He rested it across the top of the canoe. Setting his elbows on his knees, he cupped his head in his hands.

"What's the hold-up?" Juan asked. Even though it

was a bitchy question, Juan's expression wasn't half as haughty as it usually was. He seemed almost...concerned? About Theo? Impossible!

Afi turned around in his seat. "You okay, man? You look a little sea-sick."

"No," Theo moaned. This was it. He was going all in. "Lovesick, more like. I came all the way out here just to get next to you. Didn't you realize that? Couldn't you see me trying?"

"Aww!" Juan clasped his hand to his heart. "I love you too! Come here and give me a kiss!"

Afi gave Juan a playful smack with his paddle. "Shut up, you idiot. You know Theo's talking to me."

When Afi smiled, Theo felt encouraged for the first time this entire trip. "Are you two..." How should he phrase it? "Are you back together or something? I've asked around, and everyone said no, but...you seem..."

Juan chuckled and turned to smile at Afi. "We're just having fun this week."

"That was our agreement," Afi said with a nod. "We always did have great sex. It was just...other stuff...that was bad."

"I don't want to see you get hurt again." Bold move, to say it right in front of Juan's face, but he had to get that on the table. "I know how easy it is to fall for someone you loved in the past."

Afi nodded. "Thanks, man. I appreciate that."

"And I want you to know I've changed," Juan added. "I moved in with my next boyfriend right after Afi, and it was bad juju, man. Overnight it was like I became my father—and my father was not a nice man. Suddenly I was saying the things my dad used to say to my mother, acting like a total shithead. And I couldn't even see it, not while it was happening. My boyfriend picked up and left. I went off the deep end, but the way it happened I ended up talking to someone who helped me with a lot of the learned behaviours and self-loathing that made me treat guys the way I did."

Theo nodded, though he wasn't sure if he trusted Juan. The guy could charm the shorts off an entire track team if he put his mind to it. Theo knew what he'd been like back in the day. Could somebody really change so much?

"But you're right," Afi said. "I don't want to get hurt again. Juan and I agree our time has passed, but that doesn't mean we can't spend a week sucking and fucking, right?"

"I guess not…" Theo loved Afi's forgiving nature, but could he bear his crush's dalliances with an ex? "What about after this week? Do you think I could take you out or something?"

It felt strange to ask Afi on a date over Juan's shoulder, but the time was right. Now or never.

Strangely—and this really did freak Theo out a bit—Juan smiled just as widely as Afi.

"Yeah, for sure!" Afi said. "I've been hoping you'd ask. I was never sure if you were flirting with me for real, or just for laughs."

"Yeah, man," Juan chimed in. "You flirt with everyone."

Theo couldn't believe his ears! "Who, me? Since when?"

"Since forever!" Juan said, and laughed. The man had a very attractive mouth. He had great hair, too—shoulder-length and jet black. It shimmered in the sunlight almost as much as the rippling water. But Juan was way off about the flirting.

"I'm not a flirt. I can't believe you guys."

Afi shook his head. "Oh, buddy, you come on to everyone! That's why I never thought I had a chance with you."

"You do," Theo replied in earnest. "You're the only one who has a chance."

Pulling his backpack onto his lap, Juan unzipped it and brought out a string of condoms and about gallon of lube. "I hope he's not the only one. We are on vacation, after all. This is a week for fun."

Afi nodded his encouragement, but Theo wasn't exactly sure what Juan was getting at. He didn't want to guess wrong or he'd feel like an idiot.

"You mean the three of us?" Theo asked. He'd never tried it, but he liked the idea. "Together?"

"Afi and I came out here for a poke on the water. You're welcome to join in."

Theo looked quickly to Afi, who was still beaming and nodding. "It'll be great. Juan is one mean cocksucker."

No way Theo could argue there.

"Take off your swimsuit." Juan's smile was positively canine. "Let's see your cock."

Afi started to stand up, but the canoe wobbled side to side. Second-guessing himself, he sat back down with an anticipatory grin. Untying his waistband, Theo loosened the drawstring fly. He looked to Juan and then to Afi. They shared smiles and dark gazes. The seemed ready to pounce, and that made Theo feel incredibly desired. Holding tight to the sides of the canoe, he rose to his feet without rocking the boat too much. He'd been out paddling dozens of times, but he'd never fucked two guys inside a canoe. Summer was full of surprises.

Planting his feet flat at the base, Theo pushed his swim shorts clear past his knees. By the time they covered his flip flops, Juan and Afi's smirks had grown into full-blown smiles. They stared unabashedly at Theo's naked cock, and the lust in their eyes nearly knocked him off-kilter.

The summer sun felt warm against his skin, but the slight mist in the air kept him cool. These boys would get him hot—he could see it in their eyes. They seemed to drool over his body like a pair of wolverines. They wanted him—that much was clear. But who would get him first?

Theo took his cock in hand and stroked it from base to tip. Was it weird to touch himself in front of two other guys? He didn't really care. The pressure his loose fist exerted on his shaft made him shudder with anticipation.

Juan and Afi obviously enjoyed the little show he put on for them, because they slipped out of their beach clothes too. Afi kept his lifejacket on, which was probably wise, but Juan sat in the middle of the canoe in all his naked glory. He had a fine cock, that Juan. It curved upwards even more than Afi's—a build-in prostate pleaser!

So many images raced through Theo's mind—getting sucked and getting fucked, hands and tongues and cocks and holes—but nobody seemed prepared to move for fear of tipping the vessel.

"Am I just putting on a show?" Theo teased, waving his erection up and down. "Or does somebody want to suck this thing?"

They both elected to suck, and then laughed.

"You'll have plenty of opportunities to taste his monster," Juan said to Afi. "This could be my only one. He's mine."

But Juan was obviously too nervous to move in the canoe. He stretched out his hands and wriggled his fingers as if to say, "Come to me! Come here and let me suck you!"

Theo took tentative steps toward the middle of the canoe while Juan passed his sexual supplies back to Afi. If only Theo had something, anything, to hold on to...and then he felt his paddle knock softly against shins. Inspired, he picked it up and asked for Afi's as well. He used them like crutches, propping them just under his arms and setting the flat ends against the bottom of the boat. That was better. Now he felt steady, at least until Juan gripped his shaft and flicked his cockhead with the tip of his tongue—that threw Theo for a loop. He grasped the paddles and dug them down to maintain his upright position.

When Juan closed his full lips around the gleaming purple flesh of Theo's cockhead, Theo's thighs tensed. His knees went weak. Was it a good idea to thrust into Juan's mouth while standing up in a canoe? His hips didn't care. They lunged forward, filling Juan's throat with cock.

Releasing his grasp on Theo's shaft, Juan held his thighs instead. He swallowed more cock. His throat seemed to click like he was starting to gag, but he quickly recovered, sliding the length of Theo's erection out of his mouth and then back inside.

"What did I tell you?" Afi said. "Juan gives a hell of a blowjob."

Descending to his knees, Afi gripped both sides of the canoe and inched closer to Juan. When he was close enough to reach around the BJ-master's body, Afi took that cock in his fist and pumped it. Even with a mouth full of big black cock, Juan moaned and bucked into Afi's clenched fingers.

"Get your hot ass back here, mister!" he said.

Grabbing the lube from the base of the canoe, Afi greased up both hands before regaining his grip on Juan's surging erection. As Theo looked over Juan's cocksucking head, Afi ran a glistening hand down Juan's crack. Theo could almost feel that cool grease against his hole as Afi snuck a finger inside Juan's ass.

Juan groaned, sending vibrations all through Theo's body. He imagined what the three of them looked like, three levels of naked men in the middle of a lake, one fingerfucking and handjobbing, one cocksucking, and one just standing there and enjoying the view.

A surge of electricity coursed through Theo's body at the idea of being caught. What was it? Adrenaline? Lust? Anxiety? Guilty Pleasure?

What if somebody saw them? There were cottages hiding behind tree cover all around this big lake. What if every guy in every cottage had a pair of binoculars in hand? What if a hundred pairs of eyes were on them at that very moment, surreptitiously jerking off to the sight of three naked guys in a canoe? Or calling out to their partners, "Honey, you have to get a look at this!"

All wishful thinking. More likely it would be, "Faggots! Call the cops!"

Theo's heart thumped wild in his chest. "Oh god, Juan, let me fuck you!"

Afi looked up at Theo with surprise in his eyes, but that expression quickly melted into a smile as he tossed over a condom and the bottle of lube.

It seemed to take ages for his entire erection to emerge from Juan's throat. His cock just went on forever. God, he'd never been so hard. This was a whole new game, to Theo.

"Fuck me!" Juan pleaded when Theo's glistening tip finally emerged from his mouth. "Your cock is so huge it's going to tear me open, but I don't care. I want you to break me."

Maybe it was Theo's imagination, but Afi looked jealous. Even so, he backed up slowly, until his head rested against his seat at the front of the canoe. He was still wearing his puffy orange lifejacket, but maybe he was the smart one. His surging cock begged for pleasure as Juan flipped upside down on the wooden crossbar.

Juan's back shone in the summer sun. His ass was more muscle than flesh, but all Theo cared about was the puckered asshole begging to be filled.

As Juan swallowed Afi's prick, Theo fitted his proud cock with latex. He squirted so much lube down Juan's ass crack that it ran down and coated his nuts. Theo cupped them and Juan gasped. There was something tempting about those lubed-up balls. He couldn't resist kneeling down and pressing his boys against them. Juan burbled with joy as his head bobbed between Afi's legs.

Theo rested his sheathed cock in Juan's ass crack and pressed their nut sacks together. He was gentle about it, but firm in his pressure. He wanted to get off good with these guys.

When Theo leaned forward, he was just at the right height to cram his dick in Juan's puckered ass. Taking his shaft in hand, Theo pressed his cockhead to Juan's hole. It didn't ease up right away. He pressed his weight forward until that tight assring opened to let him inside.

Despite the cock in his mouth, Juan yelped when Theo entered his ass.

"Ease up," Theo told him. "Ease your ass up."

Theo caught Afi looking back and forth between the one guy sucking his dick and the other guy fucking him. They smiled when their gazes met. It didn't take long before Afi started bucking like crazy. He shrieked when Juan unzipped his lifejacket and pinched his dark nipples.

With an animal squeal, Afi bucked into Juan's face. Did he always come so fast, or was Theo's presence an extra turn-on?

"Let Juan fuck you," Theo pleaded.

Without even pulling his cock out of Juan's ass, Theo pulled back on Juan's hips. Juan must have been nervous about flipping the vessel, because his asshole clamped down hard as he crawled toward the back of the boat. In fact, Juan's ass ring milked his raging erection with such force, Theo nearly filled him with jizz then and there.

Afi was even more afraid of rocking the boat than Juan had been. Setting his shorts underneath his spent cock, he got belly down on the bottom. Juan suited up and took his bottle of lube in hand while Afi shuffled back like a worm until he was in position. Legs splayed, knees on the base of the canoe, feet up in the air, Afi raised his ass to just under the centre bar so Juan could hold on tight while he reamed that tight brown butt.

It felt dirty, naughty, and just a little cosmic when Juan shoved his dick in Afi's ass. The three of them became a chain, fucking in sequence. Theo felt almost as if Juan's cock was an extension of his own, plunging deep inside Afi's hole.

For the first few thrusts, Theo moved in time with Juan. They were totally in synch. But, after a time, it became like walking arm in arm with someone taller or smaller than yourself—the motion was stilted, and they moved in rhythms off the beat. It felt awkward, and Theo worked to regain their syncopation.

When he pummeled Juan's ass, Juan recoiled against Afi. They all bounced off one another like billiard balls smacking again and again, going off in this direction or that, and meeting in the middle. The canoe didn't seem to know how to react. It barely moved beneath them. Maybe they'd stunned it.

Theo dug down between their thighs until he grasped Juan's ball sack. Juan yelped when as Theo grabbed his long black hair. It was almost too hot to touch. He kept his fingers around tight nuts. And he thrust.

Not just thrust, but plunged his raging erection inside Juan's ass. He picked up the pace, and Juan knocked harder against Afi's sweet cheeks. Theo could only see the back of Afi's head now, but he could hear the boy swearing. "Shit, yeah. Fuck me! Fill me up with cum!"

Theo rammed Juan harder. He was the driver. He'd bring them both to orgasm, everybody at once.

"Yeah!" Afi cried as they fucked.

Juan had desperation in his voice. "Squeeze my balls. Squeeze them hard. I love that!"

Theo didn't stop squeezing nuts or pulling hair or fucking Juan's tight ass until the man started whimpering. "Oh god, I'm going to come! I'm coming! I'm going to come!"

And did he ever! He came so hard, Theo could feel it in his balls... at least, that's what Theo thought until he realized he was feeling his own ejaculation. They came together, with Afi whimpering on the bottom. And, yes, now he could feel his cockhead wading in hot cum inside Juan's whimpering hole. He loved that feeling. It was so hot in the condom that he didn't want to pull out, but the boys started to squirm. He took a load off at the back of the canoe.

"Holy Mother!" Juan sighed as he picked up his shorts from the bottom of the canoe.

Afi picked himself up, put on his bathing suit, and zipped up his lifejacket. "That was wild. I'm sweating all over."

"Yeah, me too," Theo said. "I could sure go for a dip."

One by one, they each grabbed the sides of the canoe.

"I can't believe we managed a ménage without tipping the canoe!" Juan laughed.

"Seems like kind of a shame to flip in on purpose,"

Afi said. "But…"

Theo held the paddles in place with his feet. "Ready?" he asked the guys. When they both nodded, he started the count down. "Three, two, one… go!"

BRODY AND THE BOY BENCH

It was the last thing in the world Brody expected to find. He walked Patch in the same park every day, and he'd never noticed anything untoward. But maybe that's because the bench was shielded on three sides by a thick cloak of pine trees, and for some reason faced away from the dirt path.

Of course, the bench itself isn't what had captured. Brody's attention. It was the people on the bench that really interested him. He heard their voices and stopped short, pulling Patch's leash hard enough to make the poor dog whine.

"Yeah, touch it."

A man's voice, deep and confident.

Touch what?

Brody was pretty sure he knew, but he had to see what was going on behind those trees.

"Wow, it's hard as wood." That lisping voice was distinctly male, though much higher than the first. "You've got the biggest cock I've ever seen."

The deep voice laughed at the obvious flattery, but now Brody was even more tempted to catch a glimpse of these guys. Were they naked, or fully clothed with just their dicks sticking out their open flies? That would be the way to go, Brody figured, in a public park where they might be caught at any moment. They were deep in the woods, granted, and Brody walked here every day and hardly met another soul. So, hell, maybe they were naked after all. Brody just had to find out.

"You afraid of my big black cock?" That was the deep voice again.

The higher voice let out a witchy cackle. "Honey, I'm not afraid of anything."

"Then how come you're hardly touching it? Come on, now, grab my dick."

"What does it feel like I'm doing?" the lisping boy

whined.

Deep Voice said, "Here, let me show you how it's done."

The men moaned in unison, and then went quiet. The only sound Brody could hear was the unmistakable flap of hands on dicks. Now this he had to see...

Tip-toeing between two outlying pines, Brody poked his head between branches, praying Patch would keep quiet just long enough for him to see something good. Thankfully, the carpet of needles underfoot didn't crunch the way dried leaves would have.

He could see them now, sort of. There were still branches in the way. Brody stood behind the bench, somewhat off to the side, but he could make out Deep Voice's broad shoulders and the back of the guy's bald head. Lispy had a mop of wheat-coloured hair. He seemed to be wearing a grocery store uniform.

But the two things Brody most wanted to see were blocked by the angle of the bench and the men's bodies. They were sitting mighty close, those two. Brody could tell by the motion of Lispy's right shoulder that he was jerking off Deep Voice. Curiously, both the black man's shoulders were heaving. Brody itched to get a look at what was happening on the other side of that goddamn bench. His cock stained against his jeans so hard it hurt. Why couldn't he see what he wanted to see?

"Dude, you're crushing my fingers," Lispy said in a whisper.

One of Deep Voice's shoulders stopped moving, and he shook his right hand out at his side. "How's that?"

Ahh, so that was the story. Not only had Deep Voice been playing with Lispy's dick, he'd wrapped his hand around the little guy's fist for added pressure. The very idea of a big black hand enveloping a little white hand, both jerking the guy off together, made Brody's cock strain harder against his fly. His erection had grown too damn big to stay in his pants. He needed to unzip.

"You gotta make me come fast," Lispy pleaded. "My lunch break's almost over and I gotta run all the way back to the parking lot."

"Oh, you're not leaving until I blow my load," Deep Voice shot back. That statement would have seemed threatening if the guy's tone hadn't been so playful.

"I'm gonna be late for work!" The young guy's voice sounded pinched, strained, even higher than before. He tossed his head back, and his hair danced behind the bench. There was a lot of it, and Brody wondered how those wheat-gold strands would feel tickling his thighs.

Lispy had beautiful lips, full and pink. What Brody wouldn't give to feel them wrapped around his shaft. Fuck, he needed to unzip his jeans. Why couldn't he work up the nerve?

The slap of hands on dicks grew quicker, slicker, as the men's moans evolved into groans and grunts. They were coming, both of them, and Brody didn't even have the guts to stroke his huge hard-on over his jeans. He was so afraid that if he moved, the guys on the bench would turn around. God, he'd be so embarrassed.

"Fuck, I'm gonna blow!" Lispy cried.

Deep Voice went totally in the opposite direction, booming out, "Awwww yeah!"

Their excitement was too much for Patch, who'd been perfectly quiet until that moment. The rumbling explosions made him bark, and the men both snapped their heads around. Stunned, Brody latched the young guy's gaze. He couldn't break away.

Patch wouldn't stop barking while Brody apologized, pretending he hadn't been standing there watching for the past five minutes. Thank God his cock wasn't hanging out of his pants. He ran all the way back to the parking lot.

His dick was still rock solid when he got to the car. He urged Patch into the back seat and pulled out of there as fast as his lead foot would take him. He'd never been so embarrassed in all his life. He'd never been so turned on, either. It was a bizarre combination of emotions.

Patch ran straight to his water bowl when they got home, and Brody opted for a bowl of Corn Flakes. Maybe dull foods would calm his senses and bring his raging erection down? No such luck. He paced the floor, turning on the computer, then sorting through his porn DVDs. No, nothing appealed to him. He cupped his bulge through his jeans, rubbing the head of his cock with his palm. No, that wasn't good enough. Nothing would be good enough, nothing but that goddamn bench.

He had to go. *Now*.

"Back in a while," he called to Patch, grabbing his keys but nearly forgetting to lock the door. He strained to keep from speeding all the way back to the park, and when he got to the lot he almost jumped out of the car without turning it off.

Brody walked by that secluded bench every day, but damned if he could locate it now. Where the hell had it gone? He felt like he was running in circles.

Wait... there it was! He approached slowly, peeking around the trees, but the bench was empty. Disappointment twisted his gut into knots, but what had he expected? Did he really think those two guys would still be there after all this time?

With a heavy sigh, Brody rested his weary butt on the bench and stretched his arms across the back. Closing his eyes, he concentrated on the erection pummelling his jeans. What was he going to do about that? Jerk off in the middle of the forest?

Hell, why not?

Just as Brody reached one hand down to unbutton and unzip, a voice like warm milk said, "Mind if I join you?"

Stunned, Brody covered his erection, though it was still in his pants. "Uhh... sure."

The guy was definitely a few years older. He was neat and lean, a full head of black hair dappled with greys, and striking silver beard.

"No, leave it," the man said when Brody started to move his arm off the back of the bench. "I don't mind getting cosy."

"Oh," Brody stammered. "Good."

"It's your first time, isn't it?"

"First time?" Brody felt like an idiot. He had no idea what to say.

"First time at the Boy Bench."

Brody gulped, though he wanted to laugh. "Boy Bench?"

Silver Beard smelled like a salad, the kind with chicken and mandarin oranges and sesame dressing. The aroma made Brody hungry.

"I suppose it ought to be called a Man Bench, but alliterations are fun, don't you think?" This guy was so well-spoken Brody would have been intimidated in any other setting. "You're here for a *handout*, shall we say?"

This was starting to make sense now. Brody let himself laugh. His heart stopped racing, but his dick still pounded his jeans. "You want to...? Should I...?" He never did this sort of thing. He wasn't sure how to get started.

Silver Beard peeled Brody's fingers away from his crotch and let out an impressed whistle. "We *are* eager!"

"Yeah, well..." Brody chuckled sheepishly. "I saw some guys here earlier and I couldn't get them out of my mind."

"Ahhh." Silver Beard nodded. "Yes, the Boy Bench certainly has that effect. Now whip it out. Let's have a look."

Brody was so goddamn horny he complied without question. The moment his fly was open his cock sprang out like a jack-in-the-box. He pushed his jeans down past his knees because the sharp metal teeth of his zipper made him nervous.

Silver Beard growled when Brody revealed his erection, and that sound made his cock jump like it was begging for the man's touch. He was so hard it hurt.

"Impressive." Silver Beard raised an eyebrow.

"Why don't you get started and I'll join in when the old boy is ready."

What could he say? Brody would have given a limb to feel another man's touch, but he was never one to make waves. "Okay…sure, no problem."

While Silver Beard squeezed his own crotch through fitted grey flannels, Brody wrapped his hand around his dick. He couldn't contain the deep moan that escaped his lips.

"Sounds like you've been waiting all day for that."

"Feels like I've been waiting *all year* for it!" Brody flicked beneath his cockhead, circling his thumb and index finger around his girth. Grasping that flesh, he urged it upward until it partially covered his tip. "Christ, that's good."

"Mmm." Silver Beard was hard beneath his flannels now, and he traced his hand up and down that bulging outline. "Sounds as good as it looks."

Teasing his fat tip, Brody surprised himself by saying, "It would look even better with someone else's fist wrapped around it."

With a devious chuckle, Silver Beard asked, "Did

you have anyone in mind?"

"Well, *you're* right here." Brody slipped his arm from around the suave man's shoulder and let their fingers mesh over the flannel bulge. Silver Beard's cock thwacked the fabric as they petted it together.

It was a bit of a shock when the older man kissed him. That tongue was a miracle of nature, moving in his mouth like a hurricane, and it tasted of sesame and orange. It had been ages since he'd kissed a guy with facial hair, and the grizzly tickle felt so damn good he found himself edging to the side just to get a little more.

The sound of Silver Beard's belt unbuckling and fly unzipping bolted through his body like lightning. In seconds Brody had a hard cock in each hand, and he moved closer to the man in flannel trousers, moth to flame.

Even with his eyes closed, Brody could feel the curve in Silver Beard's dick. It made him wonder what this guy was thinking—that his dick was weirdly bulbous toward the tip? That his ball hair was in bad need of a trim? That he had Corn Flakes breath?

They hadn't yet broken from their tempestuous kiss when Silver Beard gripped Brody's cock. He felt strangely protective of it for a moment, but cajoled himself into handing over his most precious possession. This was good. Now he could concentrate his full attention on giving a good hand job. Though, how could he concentrate fully when this stranger was jerking him off and kissing him, driving him into such a frenzy of lust he felt like he was drowning in it?

Brody thrust into Silver Beard's fist. Some lotion or lube would have been good, but the lack of it made this encounter all the more gritty. Brody savoured the sensation like a morsel of steak. He couldn't keep his hips down. Christ, he'd been hard for so long he just had to come. It wouldn't be long now. His thighs were already trembling and his balls were so tight against his body he thought they might jump back inside.

He moaned into Silver Beard's mouth, but had to break the kiss to cry out, "Aww yeah, man, aww yeah!"

Brody looked down just in time to see an explosion of jizz soar from his cock, arching in the forest air before landing, a wet mess in the pine needles. The bursts of cum didn't stop there, and Brody felt like his essence was being sucked from his body. His jeans were streaked with the stuff by the time he noticed he wasn't stroking Silver Beard at all. His fist was locked around the guy's dick, but he wasn't moving.

Feeling like a selfish ass, Brody started up again,

but he was too exhausted to do a great job. A little piece of him wanted to give up. And then Silver Beard started grunting like an animal and fucking his hand.

"Are you going to come?" Brody asked in disbelief. Had he really done enough to give this guy an orgasm?

Silver Beard cupped his balls with one hand, squeezing that grey-haired sac while Brody shuttled up and down the man's curved hard-on. Yes he was tired, but his arm was hell-bent on coaxing a climax out of this guy. He knew it was working when Silver Beard started panting and bucking, shoving that keen cock through Brody's clenched fist.

"Come," Brody begged. "Spill it, man. Jizz all over me."

Leaning against Brody's shoulder, Silver Beard gave one last thrust and then shuddered. Hot cream blasted from his dick. He spilled his cum all over Brody's thighs. The scorching heat from that sticky stuff made Brody's spent cock twitch.

They sat together, shoulder to shoulder, for a long, dazed moment. It took a while for Silver Beard to catch his breath. When he did, he chuckled and asked, "Did you enjoy your first time on the Boy Bench?"

That had to be a rhetorical question.

"Trust me," Brody said, "I'll be back soon."

SWIMMING IN THE RAIN

"We called these 'thongs' when I was a kid."
Ernie laughed as they slogged through rivulets in the
beach sand. "Nobody calls 'em that anymore."

Quinn nodded, trailing brightly-coloured pool
noodles behind him. "We always called them flip-
flops."

"Yeah, I guess we did, too." It seemed so long
ago, the beach vacations of youth. It wasn't really,
though—twenty years, maybe? Twenty years wasn't
such a long time. Still, Ernie felt old at thirty, more so
because Quinn was only twenty-three. And *hot*.

God, was Quinn ever a good-looking guy, with that
skin of Polynesian gold. A little on the short side, but
strong and built without looking grossly over-muscled.

He'd cut his silky black hair just last week, and Ernie couldn't decide if he'd liked it better longer or if this funky new do was more his style.

Already, Ernie missed running his hands through those lustrous strands while Quinn kneeled to give him head. It always made Ernie feel so powerful when he could wrap that thick hair around his fist, pulling tight, guiding the motion of Quinn's mouth on his hard cock. Quinn would yelp a little, the sound high in his throat as he sucked Ernie's dick, sucked harder the longer they went at it, until Ernie just filled his mouth with cum. Everything was so good when they were together.

Now Ernie shielded his eyes, his dick pulsing with the memories. "My dad always used to say a storm was the best time to swim."

Quinn did the same. "I hope to hell he was right about that, because I'm freezing my ass off in this downpour."

That thought, planted in Ernie's mind, made him shiver. Suddenly he was so cold he wanted to call it off and head back to curl up under a warm blanket. Quinn's body was hot enough to keep them both toasty all through the night.

"Well?" Quinn asked, kicking off his flip-flops in

the rain-hardened sand. "We going in or what?" He held all three pool noodles under one arm.

Ernie hoped like hell he was remembering those halcyon swims in the rain as they'd truly been. His memory had them pegged as warm baths, isolated from the less-hardy vacationing masses who had all returned to their tents or trailers or cabins or wherever they'd come from. As he looked around the abandoned beach, he felt certain he and Quinn were about to have the time of their lives.

Tossing his swim trunks in the sand, Ernie raced down the stretch of beach, beckoning Quinn to follow him into the water. He sensed the young hottie traipsing down the wet sand behind him, dragging those silly noodles.

When Ernie's toes met the water's lapping edge, he shrieked and backed away. Quinn stopped behind him, and when he turned to find the guy naked except for a shell-bead necklace, his whole body heated to a simmer.

"What's wrong?" Quinn asked, his brow furrowing. "It's cold, isn't it? I told you so!"

For a moment, Ernie couldn't say anything at all. The thick surge of Quinn's erection rendered him speechless. Ernie loved Quinn's dick—the way its fat cockhead leaned a little to the left, the sheer beauty of the thing even when it rested limp against that dark pillow of balls—but to the best of his recollection, he'd never seen the thing naked out of doors. He couldn't believe what a huge turn-on it was to be nude, with the waves briskly licking at his heels.

Without so much as glancing behind himself, Ernie backed into the tepid water. The temperature seemed to improve as the lake devoured his legs. It wasn't until the water reached his thighs that he reached down to shield his cock, finding it heavy and hard with arousal. For some reason, he was surprised by this, like his dick wasn't an inextricable portion of his anatomy.

"Holy fuck," Ernie said as he touched himself. He still couldn't take his eyes off Quinn. "Look how hard you got me."

Raindrops pinged off the disrupted glass of the water's surface, wetting the dark hair surrounding Ernie's dick. It wasn't a particularly windy day, and the downpour seemed to keep the waves at bay. Quinn approached, pool noodles floating at the water's surface, hard cock slapping his belly. Dark lust set in, like deep red garnets at the back of Quinn's eyes. Ernie knew that was an expression made just for him.

It wasn't easy to feel so confident with a younger man, but his self-consciousness faded away as Quinn came closer. "I sure am glad nobody's around."

"Yeah?" Ernie cocked his head, pulling absently on his erection. "And why's that?"

Quinn took another step forward while Ernie took a step back. "Because this way we can do whatever we want together and nobody's going to complain."

Raindrops meandered down Quinn's naked chest, making his skin gleam, even in the absence of sunlight. Quinn was never dull, even on grey and cloudy days like this. When he reached silently for Ernie's cock, what could Ernie do but let him have it?

Quinn's touch shocked Ernie's system even more than the water had. He was sure his cock doubled in size as an instant reaction. Even his balls throbbed like they were ready to blow, but Ernie wouldn't allow it. He tensed his thighs, clenching his butt, telling himself not to let it happen, not so soon. There was still so much he wanted to do.

Ernie let the lake swallow his ass and his dick both at once, and the warmth was a surprise. Once he was in up to his nipples, the water felt positively pleasant. Even the rain falling on his head felt warmer now, and

Quinn just followed along without releasing his hold on Ernie's erection.

"Trying to get away from me?" Quinn asked with a smirk.

"Yeah right." Ernie moved in closer, so encumbered by water that he had to hop rather than step. He'd always imagined this is what it would feel like to walk on the moon: bouncing, feeling light and feeling pressure both at once. When he was close enough to feel Quinn's hot breath on his lips, he said, "I'll never let you get away."

"Is that so?" Quinn was so cute when he teased like this. "I've got my hand wrapped around your cock, but Ernie-boy, you've got no hold on me."

With a mocking laugh, Quinn started swimming in the rain. He had all three pool noodles tucked beneath his chest and his feet splashed behind him like a child learning to swim, but was he ever fast! Within seconds he'd moved beyond Ernie's grasp. Ernie reached out for his big toe, thinking maybe he'd be able to capture it, but Quinn's entire body eluded him. How he missed that firm hand stroking his dick—missed it already!

"I won't let you escape, little man!" Ernie dove underwater, and the total immersion was at first a shock to his system, but his temperature soon regulated. When it did, he realized there were levels of warmth down there. The closer he swam to the sandy lake bed, the cooler the water became. When he surged back up for air, the water at the surface was super-warm, just like he remembered from childhood. He dove down deep and swam like a fish, fast enough to catch Quinn up and grab him by the ankle.

"Told you I'd never let you go," Ernie teased.

Quinn was still kicking when he asked, "You think you've got me beat? Well, who's the one with all the floaties?"

Rolling in the water, with the pool noodles at his back, Quinn floated easy as pie at the surface of the lake. It was only then that Ernie realized how far out they'd come, and he was the one stuck treading water.

"Can I have a noodle, Quinn?" He felt like a child asking like that, but he was getting tired fast.

"Hmmm…" Quinn stroked the humble beginnings of a beard before letting his hand trail down his chest. His erection seemed to have grown in length, girth, and fortitude, and once Quinn's hand found it, it grew some more. "I don't know. Maybe. Depends what you can do for me."

Out of breath already, Ernie nodded. "I can help you out there, for starters."

"Oh, and that's just for starters, eh?" Quinn smirked and opened his legs wide, allowing the two pink noodles to roll behind his back all the way down until they reached just past his butt. Ernie doggie-paddled between those firm thighs, mesmerized as much by the rain pooling in Quinn's navel as the droplets sizzling against the head of Quinn's cock. Steam rose from that hot body, like sundrenched wood. The drops felt huge as they pummelled Ernie's scalp. He could feel each one through his sopping wet hair.

Swimming between Quinn's thighs, Ernie leaned his weight on the floating noodles. Quinn still had one, the yellow one, underneath his shoulders. His arms stretched out across it. Ernie tried not to see it as a crucifixion pose but, naturally, the more he tried not to see that, the more he saw it. So instead, he focused his attention on the slight slant of Quinn's cock. Nobody else around. That big boy was all his.

"What are you waiting for, a written invitation?" Quinn wiped droplets from his forehead, where his wet hair was plastered to his skin. "I could just swim away and take my noodles with me."

Ernie cupped his hands around Quinn's muscular butt cheeks and squeezed them hard. "You're not going anywhere, my fabulous friend."

"Fabulous, am I?" Quinn eased his sinking pelvis up from the water. "So why aren't you sucking my fabulous cock, eh?"

Rain pelted Ernie's back harder in that moment, driving him down to meet Quinn's shaft. The length of it lay flat against his stomach. It curved away from the pond at his navel, but rose like magic when Ernie bent to swallow it whole.

Drifting on the water, Ernie licked the solid length of Quinn's shaft. Quinn shuddered, and the pool in his belly button quaked complicity. His cock tasted fresh like rain, which was both disappointing and enthralling. The downpour seemed to wash Quinn's precum away just as fast as his pearly pink cockhead could pump it out. Ernie loved the taste of that stuff, the salty sweetness that was both characteristic of all men and singular to Quinn.

Ernie brought Quinn's satin cockhead into his mouth. That great golden torso leapt from the water's surface before he'd howled, "Fuck, man! Oh God, yeah…"

Before today, Ernie had never gone swimming naked. The underwater surge of his cock was an altogether unfamiliar sensation. The lake's wet warmth caressed his dick with the same envious care he now took in sucking Quinn's hard-on. He had to kick his feet to keep his body afloat, and it was the delicate sort of ballet that would fold in on itself if he thought too much about it.

So, instead of thinking, he simply acted, sucking Quinn's cock hard and fast. He took in mainly just the tip and a portion of the shaft until he felt Quinn's hand pressing down on his head.

"Take it all," Quinn was saying, his voice strained and yet clearly audible over the shattering rain. "Suck my dick, man!"

Ernie offered sloppy licks followed by deep lunging swallows, all the while holding tight to that firm ass. He felt a tightness all though his body, because he knew the kind of swirling pleasure it must be generating in Quinn's core. Even in warm water, Ernie's balls strained and drew in close to his body. What about Quinn's?

When Ernie bent to investigate, opening his mouth wide and taking them both in at once, those hairy sacs were hard as golf balls. They'd drawn up flush to the base of Quinn's cock like they were trying to get as far away from the water as possibly.

But there was water everywhere. It was falling from the sky. There was no escape, not even in the warmth of Ernie's mouth—though Quinn's balls seemed not to mind it in there. Those rock-hard nuts expanded against Ernie's tongue until he was just about choking on them. Quinn's dark hair tickled the back of his throat. When he breathed in through his nose, enough lake water entered his system that he imagined himself drowning while he sucked his boyfriend's balls. What a way to go!

"Fuck, yeah!" Quinn grabbed his cock and stroked just below the tip, teasing that ridge. The satin flesh of his cockhead had gone from pink to red and now bordered on purple. Ernie wondered if he should take his mouth away from Quinn's balls and suck his cock instead.

When Quinn hollered, "Suck my balls, man! Suck 'em both!" that gave Ernie his answer.

Quinn's hand moved on that hard cock so fast Ernie worried he might get hit in the face with those quick-moving knuckles. They were both splashing now, kicking and writhing in the water, trying desperately to stay afloat on a grand total of three pool noodles. With his mouth full of balls, Ernie obviously couldn't speak, but he mumbled and moaned, and Quinn seemed to appreciate the vibrations.

"I'm gonna come!" Quinn cried. His hair was sopping when he lifted his head to watch.

Ernie's hand moved so fast it was hardly more than a blur. He turned his attention to Quinn's face, screwed up into an aroused press of features. Ernie wanted more than anything else in the world to see Quinn come. He sucked relentlessly on the mass of balls inside his mouth.

All at once, thick white ropes of cum soared from Quinn's cock. Stream after stream erupted from his dick, landing across Quinn's side and slipping into the water. Ernie tried to extract Quinn's massive balls from his mouth, but they seemed huger than ever. It took some doing.

"Okay, it's my turn now." Ernie's dick was so engorged he knew he'd come the second Quinn's full lips touched his cockhead. "Suck it underwater."

"What?" Quinn's eyes widened, but he was smiling. "You're going to drown me, aren't you?"

"Not if you make me come," Ernie teased.

With a sly shrug, Quinn sank in the water, leaving Ernie to grab all the pool noodles. First he felt Quinn's strong hands grasping his thighs, and then those familiar lips met his tip. Oh God, he could have blown his load right then, but he wanted to feel the warmth between Quinn's lips, if only for a moment.

And, sure enough, a moment was all it took. The wet heat of Quinn's mouth enveloped his dick almost entirely. One big suck was enough. It was like Quinn was drinking his jizz through a straw, that's how easily he made Ernie come.

The sensation was swift, but tremendous, like nothing else Ernie had ever experienced. He was glad to have these floaties keeping him above water, because without them he'd be down below the surface by now.

The blast of jizz down Quinn's throat took all Ernie's energy along with it.

Ernie sensed some difference in the atmosphere, and when he looked around he realized the rain had stopped. "Would you look at that!" he said when Quinn surfaced. "Maybe we should head in before the sun comes out."

"You're going to have to carry me," Quinn teased,

floating on the calm water. Ernie knew exactly how he felt. "God, I came so fucking hard. You're a miracle worker, you know that?"

"So are you!" Ernie gazed at that godlike form. "I'm so lucky."

A keen smirk bled across Quinn's lips as he started to paddle toward shore. "Let's go back to bed and find out just how lucky you can get!"

The End

WANT MORE?
TRY:

Caged and Contused
By G.R. Richards

Four gay BDSM tales from the manic mind of G.R. Richards.

Fuck in a Truck: In the 1960's, when New York's gay clubs were raided weekly, clever guys got their asses to the meat-packing district for filthy all-night orgies. In the trucks, anything goes.

Webcam Willy: Willy's just another university student who likes to jerk off with strangers via webcam. He's a voyeur and exhibitionist all rolled into one. As much as he loves getting off in front of other guys, he loves being told what to do even more.

The Feel of Steel: Big Boy's sub had a cock with a mind of its own until Big Boy slapped a chastity devise on it. But that old plastic cock cage was an eyesore and it never did fit right. Time they switch to a gleaming steel cock lock.

Daddy Jens: Jens can't stand his son's friends. When they traipse into his house uninvited, he tells them to get lost, but Cooper and Logan aren't going anywhere. Is it time for the muscle daddy to tame them? Because Daddy Jens sure knows how to put a couple sk8er boys in their places.

Excerpt from **Caged and Contused:**

From "The Feel of Steel"

Steel was my reward.

I could see the pride gleaming in Big Boy's dark coffee eyes. Yes, he scolded me, chastised me, even punished me when I was naughty—I deserved it then—but he also encouraged me when I was good. And lately, I'd been very good.

That's why he suited me up with the stainless steel cock lock. He knew the old plastic one was uncomfortable. It didn't fit right. It was just large enough that it let me get erections, and there were even a few times when old habits turned me on so bad I ejaculated on my computer chair. That wasn't supposed to happen. There was no joy in it, for me.

Big Boy made me clean up after myself. His reactions to my misdeeds were highly parental. He never got angry when I slipped up. He'd say he was "disappointed with my behavior," and he'd take Friday night away from me. He was right to do so. I didn't deserve the pleasure.

Big Boy had a good reason for caging my cock. From the time I started working from home, my dick prevented me from accomplishing anything. My dick, in combination with the abundance of internet porn, I should say. I'd open a file, stare at the damn thing for a few minutes, and then open my internet browser and start watching sweet slave boys sucking off guys in leather harnesses.

I'd reach inside my sweats and pull out my hard cock. I'd tug on it, jerking off until I came all over the underside of my computer desk. It was a mess down there. Porn was my compulsion. Work got shifted to the backburner. I'd masturbate the day away, and have nothing to show for it but my exhaustion. I nearly lost my job.

Until I met Big Boy, I never realized there was such a simple solution to my problem. I needed to give control of my cock over to somebody else. That was it. That was the miracle cure.

WANT EVEN MORE?
TRY:

Banging the Boy Band
By G.R. Richards

From pairs to threesomes to big groups of guys, the boys in these six sex stories can't help getting hardcore.

In *One for the Money*, a group of construction workers jerk off for a pot of cash. In *Two for the Show*, a kinky couple puts on a hot fetish performance for paying customers. *Second Hand Porn* gets a first-hand look at two coworkers swapping men's magazines, while the gambler in *Grinder* pays a huge fee to enter a high stakes poker game. *Don't Look Around* takes a hardcore look at domination and eye contact, but the gay divorcé in *Banging the Boy Band* has the most fun of all when he gets down and dirty with the barely-legal teens in his daughter's favorite guy group.

These boys like it hot and hard: hands, mouths, and more!

EXCERPT:

"Bad!" Mo roared. "Bad, bad, bad boy!"

Before Jared could ask what he'd done wrong, Mo was hauling him to his feet, tossing him back against the bed. When he met Mo's gaze, he knew at once. He'd closed his eyes. He'd looked away. Exactly what he shouldn't have done.

"I'm sorry," Jared said.

"You know what you did?" Mo was heading to the closet, opening the door, pulling something out...

"I closed my eyes," Jared said. "I'm sorry."

"That's right." Mo showcased the instrument of doom. It was a single bamboo cane, thinner than his little finger.

"Holy Jesus..." Jared had never seen it before, but the sight made him shiver.

Wrapping one hand around his massive erection, Mo approached Jared slowly. "And this ain't for your ass."

Jared wasn't sure if Mo was referring to his big black cock or to the bamboo switch. Maybe both?

"What's it for?" Jared asked, leaning back against the bed.

Mo's eyes were burning. In the periphery, Jared could just see his hand stroking his cock in a slow and regimented fashion. Mo was so controlled. He wasn't just controlling. He had an amazing amount of self-discipline.

When the bamboo came crashing down, Jared jolted back against the bed. He heard it before he felt it. Even after the rod made contact with his shaft, his mind didn't work fast enough to process the pain. That was slow to follow.

He stood there, dazed, watching Mo's hand move like a stealth fighter. It wasn't until the bamboo switch fell again that a streak of lightning pain shot through him. Christ, it hurt. Blinding pain.

A white flash crossed his field of vision and the bamboo fell again. His dick blazed. It hurt so much he wanted to curl down to the floor and hug himself tight. But he didn't. He stood at the ready.

ABOUT G.R. RICHARDS

There's a reason guys growl for G.R. Richards Erotica. You would never know it by the love of public television documentaries and great food in high-end restaurants, but G.R. Richards pens some of the world's steamiest guy-on-guy stories.

Be on the lookout for Richards' hot short stories, including **Junk, Vintage Toys for Lucky Boys, Behind the Scenes, We the Bus People, Behind the Scenes, Devil's Eyes,** and many more. Looking for something a little longer? Check out Amber Allure for novellas like **The Brothers of Hogg's Hollow, Birds of a Feather, Camp Fluke** and **Profound in his Silence.** Short story collections are also available from Excessica Publishing.

Richards is also a contributor to **Men at Noon, Monsters at Midnight** (STARbooks), **Skater Boys** (Cleis Press), **When a Man Loves a Man, Bad Boys** and **Boy Fun** (Xcite Books), and a variety of e-anthologies from Constable and Robinson.

http://www.grrichards.webs.com/

CPSIA information can be obtained at www.ICGtesting.com
Printed in the USA
BVOW03s0355090914

366052BV00013BA/190/P